I0768388

THE HAND

New Edition

Chislene Lora

THE HAND
Copyright © 2025 Chislene Lora.

No part of this publication may be reproduced, distributed, or transmitted in any form or by any means, including photocopying, recording, or other electronic or mechanical methods, without the prior written permission of the publisher, except in the case of brief quotations embodied in reviews and certain other non-commercial uses permitted by copyright law.

ISBN 978-1-967362-53-0 (Paperback)
ISBN 978-1-967362-54-7 (Ebook)
ISBN 978-1-967362-55-4 (Hardcover)

Printed in the United States of America

Contents

Chapter - 1

It all started when this cop arrested my oldest son and then I decided to seduce him not because he arrested him but because his back looked nice ☺. I asked the officer why my son is being arrested and he didn't respond. Then I asked again and when he spoke with that deep voice my entire body shocked and I just walked away. It was freezing cold and I had a t-shirt with my black pajamas. He came to the neighborhood for a second time the following day and I was coming up the block with my oldest son who was carrying my grocery bags. THE MAN IN BLUE as I named him, was kneeling on the building stair with one leg up and facing the kids who were not from the neighborhood. I kind of liked the way he was standing so I decided to look back and he was looking at my bottom. He was not expecting me to look so he opened his eyes wide when I looked and then I looked again backwards and looked at his eyes and he stood up straight. I walked to my building and I looked back. I made sure that he knew I was interested. I just loved those wide eyes he has it really caught my full attention. I told my oldest son on our way to the apartment, "I will be surprised if he doesn't ask for me". It was a Friday evening and I was doing my PhD assignment and my son came inside the apartment screaming. He sounded happy and my oldest son said, Mom guess who is asking for you? In my head I was thinking THE MAN IN BLUE but didn't say anything because I didn't want my son to become upset. My oldest son said mom can you believe the cop called my name "Rafael" and I'm looking, and it was him and with three other cops. The cop asked my son about me and my son became very upset and expressed to him, "You're a baster". The cop started asking around for me and stopped my son on a Friday evening to ask, the four cops started laughing. The last thing I had in mind was that this was going to become a nightmare. A nightmare that was going to give me headaches, stress, neighborhood problems with the drug dealers and family problems.

It all started when I first saw this cop. I fell in love with his back, I asked, "Excuse me why is my son getting arrested? And no one spoke. Then, another officer spoke and said, "He was smoking pot in the building". I said, "He got arrested for that" and the officer with the great back said well that is illegal, with a deep voice. He didn't have to say that twice because it was like love at first sight and I wanted to keep seeing him to maybe one day date but unfortunately, I'm a dreamer and many times things don't come true. He kept coming around and I started coming downstairs because I said, "I am going to seduce him for putting my son in jail for some non-sense when there is an unresolved murder in the neighborhood. I did, well I thought I seduce him. He kept coming around and I kept going to the corner store, but it was to see him. He didn't know that, I think at the end he thought I was doing illegal activities. How innocent can he be not to realize when a woman is interested in him. Anyways, I kept playing the game. I kept going out to see him. I started standing in front of the building and socializing with a friend from across the streets. Things didn't go so well with her I'm not sure why, but she started focusing on the negatives. Then we just lost contact and stopped talking. I'm a blessing to many people's life and I want the best for everyone. My oldest brother started calling me and giving me advices to stay away from people who were in a lower level than I was because many times there is jealousy unfortunately. I confine in my oldest brother and I tell him everything that is happening to me. I made it clear that I wanted my family blessed and nothing else. He tells me, there is one of them in here let me speak to him. After all this drama, I decided to exclude many people out of my life because I'm busy trying to continue to achieve my goals.

Does anyone believe in Love at first sight? Well I have to say I do, but this time is different. This cop, who I call THE MAN IN BLUE; came inside the store and he bonded with me by touching my upper arm with his arm. I don't know what he did, but he should have never turned on a fire he wasn't going to turn off. Then he stood inside the store facing me and I'm looking at him all turned on and in the mood. I noticed something changed in me and that was just great because I felt different. I just couldn't speak. I was mute, completely mute. Then my pastor walks inside the store catches me starring at the cop up and down and I became more nervous. I started stuttering and my pastor noticed, and THE MAN IN BLUE noticed. He saw that I started stuttering so he stepped outside. I was so embarrassed but hey I was single so in my eyes it was okay to stare. THE MAN IN BLUE went outside, and he was just staring at his phone looking down and then he went to his car and waited for me to pass through, but I just couldn't stop looking at him and he was looking at me too. The next few days went by and he came through in a car and swiped my face from left to right starring at his eyes. Things became violent not with THE MAN IN BLUE but with the young adults from the neighborhood. To release some of the stress me and my cousin decided to start walking and we started immediately. One person came up to me and asked if I had slept with the cop that he was going to take out information from me. I became so upset because I felt as if my life was being controlled.

I thought after doing something great with my life things were going to get better, but things seem harder and more confusing. So, I'm in the middle of a war. The war of my life and I ask myself; how did I get myself in the middle of this situation? It all started when I saw this cop and those round eyes, and his black hair just pulled me inn. In a way I'm happy that I met him because I'm kind of entertained in a good way but in the other hand he never comes up to me to speak to me or says anything to me. He has been very protective and follows me everywhere, but no man can talk to me because he gets jealous. I don't know where this cop came from, but I think maybe it was an angel from heaven. God knew I needed protection and that I was being intimidated outside in the streets. I'm in a stage of my life where I don't understand what is happening. This experience is truly like a movie. Everything is confusing, and nothing makes sense and I'm 39 years going to 40 years of age. I thought by this age things were going to be simpler. I never thought I would go through this crisis in my life, "Why me". It's like I just want to run away from everything because I don't want to deal with it. I want to be happy and enjoy this time of my life but how can I, when my life right now is a big (?). I ask myself, what must I do to feel and be happy.

This is a night mare I am having well, at least it feels like it. Everything started as a game with THE MAN IN BLUE and it turned dangerous. Maybe he knew this was going to become dangerous but at least I didn't. At the time, I felt good because I knew THE MAN IN BLUE was interested in me and I was interested in him but when things started becoming dangerous I became scared. What does that have to do with me. One of the things that gets me upset is when people think I'm ignorant and I'm not.

Chapter–2

IN LOVE WITH THOUGHT OF BEING IN LOVE WITH THE MAN IN BLUE

THE MAN IN BLUE is always present and if he is not there he leaves his team to protect me. It feels good, but I have never experienced or have been used to this wonderful feeling, so it feels new and excellent. People see all the attention THE MAN IN BLUE is giving me, and they just hate it; especially women. They start treating me different and with disrespect and it makes me laugh because I 'm the one suffering here in silent. He is always there and yes, we are connected because he always senses when I'm in danger or scared. I fell in love with him and I feel unconditionally crazy for him and I named him, "THE MAN IN BLUE". He is there when he gets upset with me and he is there when he is happy with me. I have had dreams, great dreams with this man who is my LOVE. He is always around, or inside a car making sure I'm safe, it is an unimaginable dream, but it is not a dream this is a true story. This stage of my life is a New Beginning, a New Beginning because I feel good. A New Beginning because and it is my job as the character of my life and book to make me and THE MAN IN BLUE the protagonist of this book. It is my job to make myself happy and take care of me. If I don't take care of me who will take care of me. It is hard to date or be with The Man in Blue because many people hate him.

My New Beginning started when I met THE MAN IN BLUE. It has been challenging like I said but the LOVE he gives me surpasses all the issues, drama, and problems I have been experiencing in my life. I feel as if I cannot live without him anymore, I feel attached to him in a way that my heart won't beat unless he is around. This is a great time in my life and I thank God for it because I have suffered so much in life. THE MAN IN BLUE has taught me how to be stronger. When he is around he makes me strong and I feel as if I can keep moving forward in life. The moral of the story is that I'm in Love with this man. Life has become complicated and I'm thinking a lot. I still have a lot of thinking to do because is it worth going through this for Love. Life is precious and so is Love. Today for the new year's I went outside looked at the ski which was very beautiful by the way and I decided to walk even more positively. God made everything in the world and everything looks beautiful to me. I look at things and I see things different. I see life different because its clearer. Everything looks clear and wonderful. Today is a new year and in this new year's, my goal is to live a positive life. To live a healthier life and that is my goals for this year 2019. I will be treating myself more and I will be doing more self-care. Come on, just go out and take care of you. Love who you're and enjoy yourself because one day life will end and its over for this world. So, there are a few questions that I'm going to ask you personally. What are you doing to stay out of trouble? What are you doing for self-care? What are you doing for yourself overall? If you like music, go do that. If you like singing, go do that. If you enjoy hiking, then go do that? Go on vacation. Do what you love to do because it makes your inner self feel better. Before I use to take care of other people before taking care of myself but after all the negative experiences I have been through it has changed my thinking. My children laugh at me when I say that I will like to be 100 years old. I laugh too because I'm serious about turning 100 years old before I decease. I'm not playing ☺.

There is so much violence on the streets and in the world overall. People don't make it easier, they make it harder because they enjoy negativity. Negativity is not good and it's not healthy, so the question is which side are you on, the negative side or the positive side? It's good to live a healthier life and to do positive things in life because that itself makes people feel good. Staying away from negative people and socializing with positive peers is healthy and it helps a person maintain a positive energy. Negativity will always follow you, but you know what, walk away from it. Keep negativity away from your life because it's not healthy. When a person does negative things that negative thing will follow them for the rest of their life three times; and it will even hunt your loved one. Then, if anything negative happens to you or your family, you want to blame other people. Motivate yourself to do positive things and move forward in life. You don't need no one to motivate you, motivate yourself. You can do it. Many people don't want to take care of themselves before getting into a relationship or before they start caring for other people. Take care of yourself first and then worry about someone else. Trust me when a person feels overwhelmed or stressed there will be a time when people are not going to be present for you. You will have to take time and work on yourself. When a person has problems, people will run away from you but when they have problems they want you to help them. Remember you must take care of yourself first. I'm a big believer in self-care. Self-care if so important and every week I do something positive to motivate myself. I do positive things to motivate myself because that means a lot to me. Again, if you do not take care of yourself then who will take care of you??? I'm a big believer in motivation and in doing positive things for yourself because that is big and powerful. I took the train today to go downtown Manhattan and I felt so free. There was an old man inside the train and he had different animals in the cart. He had colorful birds, a black cat, two white birds, and other animals. Seeing those animals was just beautiful and it made me laugh because that is what life is about laughter, loving and having fun. Fun is good and good is fun because it is healthy for the soul. I love walking because walking is healthy, and it is a great exercise for the body.

Getting away from all the negative things in my neighborhood feels so good, it feels so relaxing and I'm free right now. My goal is to move to my own apartment and become free. I'm an independent woman because I had to depend a lot on just myself to get back on my feet. We suffer too much in life, so it is important to take care of yourself because that feels great. Some people experience traumas and crisis in their lives. That is why it is so important to live a positive, and healthy life. If someone does anything bad to you don't avenge them, walk away from them. Walking away from negativity is a better choice. Run from negativity because it is not good energy. Rights now I am in Florida running away from all the headaches and all the issues in my neighborhood. I don't know what happened to THE MAN IN BLUE, but he hates me. I do not know what happened or what I did wrong. I'm so confused. The question that I have is, why hurt me? Why use the people I love to hurt me? Why me? What did I do to you? You don't see me competing with anyone. I don't compete, I am just me. This is who I am. I am Natural, this is me, "A True Queen". I'm not going to change, this is who I am. Oh do I love myself? "Yes, I do". I'm a great and an ASOME person. I don't need anyone to motivate me or to feel good about myself; to know who I am. I was born by myself and I will die by myself. I only need God. My kids love me, my grandson loves me, and they need me; so, I must be strong for them and for myself. I think I am a little hard headed and very independent, but I thought being an independent woman was a great thing. I thought that was what men Loved, a great independent woman. Well, I am heading back to New York City lets see what life bring me after a nice and sweet vacation.

Chapter–3

A NEW BEGINNING

I am back in my apartment and the neighborhood is quiet everyone seems to be just living their life and taking it easy as it should be. Me I am looking for the man in blue and he is no where to be found. So, I decided to close that chapter in my life while it lasted. So, one day I am walking, and I see a cop's car and its him. He is starring at me from the corner of the streets, and he finally approaches me and starts talking to me. I almost fainted, we had a conversation about where I was and my vacation. We then decided to go out on a date to talk more. It was time for the date, and I dressed in the best clothes I had, and he looked stunning. W e were both happy to finally meet after all that drama I went through. We spoke about our family and our children. We spoke about the day he arrested my son and he apologized to me and then we laughed about it because we were both interested in each other. He told me we would be dating more because he wanted to get to know me better and I agreed. I met his family, and he met my family, and we dated several times. We finally kissed, and he was kissing my neck, we made love and next thing you know I feel a bite. I moved away from him, and he says sorry, but I was bleeding, so I left home, and he followed me to make sure I arrived home well. In my head I am thinking OMG he bites me on my neck what now. I go home and take a shower and I go to my room. He texts me but I am scared so I ignore his texts and I finally go to sleep. I have a nightmare about vampires eating me and me becoming a vampire them I wake up scared. I decided not to go outside since I was not working for a while and then I finally miss him, so I decide to go outside. He is inside the cop car waiting for me to go outside all these days and finally here I come. He texted me and I replied and said Hi to him. It was scary but funny at the same time. I went to my aunts' home for a while and when I came outside again, he was gone. Or maybe watching me from another corner. I went home and he texted me to make sure I was home. I replied and told him I was home. I then went to the bathroom to look at my neck and the marks were gone no marks at all when I had to holes on my neck and there was blood coming out from the holes. I was happy the holes were gone, and I was wondering if I was maybe intoxicated with something with all these diseases in this world. He texts me again and stated that he wants to see me in person. I was scared but I did miss him, so I said yes. We met in the park in central park so since he was a cop a was not scared plus there were other police cars around. I figured he is not going to bite me this time because I will scream. We met and we spoke and nicely he approached me. He told me not to be scared that he is protective over me, and he would never harm me. He told me he is different, and he wanted to show me what he meant by that. Then he took out his fangs and showed me his vampire teeth. I cried but I told him I was not scared because I loved him, and I could live without him. He told me to show him my neck and I did then he stated, yes it cleared right away" I said, "Yes". He asked for permission to bite me again and I stated, "Yes please bite me". H e bite me and the blood was dripping through my clothes, and I heard him sucking my blood and I felt no pain. I felt love, passion, no fear, and fire through my blood. Then he stopped and he put me in his cop car which was parked inside of central park, and he drove me home. There I was thinking OMG he bites me again I am I going to transform to something different then what I was a human being. He asked me if I had the energy to walk upstairs by myself and I told him, "Yes", that I was strong. I walked upstairs and I was dizzy he was just looking at me from outside to make sure I did not faint. I went straight to my bed and fell to sleep. I thought I was gong to die because I felt fire running through my blood as if it were infected. I was scared but brave when I was with him. At one point I opened my eyes and I thought I saw him in my room, but I was so weak I closed my eyes again and went to sleep. I woke up the next morning and he had text me to see if I was okay and I was simply fine, so I text back. I went to the mirror to look at myself and I felt different a little paled face and no bite marks on my neck. My brother offered me food, but I did not want to eat I was thirsty instead. I made myself a banana and strawberry shake, but it was terrible I could not understand it was my favorite drink. I still drank it but then my stomach started hurting me. I text that to him and he told me I had to be in a special diet and that we would talk about it when we meet again. That meeting date arrived, and we meet in central park again and it was amazing we kissed, and he gave me some of his blood and I drank, and I felt so good when I drank his blood it tasted fresh. He told me he was a vampire and that he chooses me to be next to him for the rest of his life and that I was going to live for many years, and I was crying because my family and children were going to pass away before I die. He explained that in our world there were others that like to challenge them, him, and his family and now me. He told me to cry that it was normal, but their will come one time where I will have no more tiers because everyone that I loved will pass on. I wanted to go home because I cried so much that my face was swollen. I did not sign up for this I told him, and he stated I choose you because we fell in love at first sight. Sorry it had to be you, but I love you and you are the one. I told him I wanted to go home because I felt tired. So, he took me home and I rested again. I was very tired lately but what I did not know was that there was one more bite for me to truly transform. That bite was coming but this one had to be in my room because the third was the worst bite. The night of the bite came, and I made sure I had taken a shower and I was well dressed, with perfume on and that my pajamas looked proper. I decided to fall asleep to feel less pain, but I could not sleep just thinking about the bite. He finally showed up in my room it was about 3:00AM in the morning my brother was out sleeping after having a few beers and my children were not home. My grandson was fast a sleep in the other room. He approached me and I was shivering from fear. He told me in my ears do not be scared because I love you and he kissed me on my cheek. He then touched my hair and bite me on my neck and I felt the blood coming out of my neck and I through to myself OMG I will never die this is scary to be alive for so many years. H e kept draining my blood off my body and then he stopped, and I felt to sleep. When I woke up the next morning, I was really paled white. No marks on my neck and in love with THE MAN IN BLUE. His name was Marcus by the way. Marcus was the love of my life and I'm thirsty for some blood I must text him. I text him and tell him to teach me how to fetch for blood and he replied yes, his blood then we laughed over the phone. He wanted me to go meet his family again because I needed to learn a lot of things that they needed to teach me. So, I went to meet his family and they welcome me into their world. It was amazing I was running with them in central park, and I ran so fast it was incredible. We bought blood from the hospital blood bank and that is how we fed our thirst. So, I asked Marcus how he felt when he drank my blood and he stated like never in his life because he drinks blood from the blood bank and its not the same as drinking a human being's blood. I asked him if other people knew they existed and he expressed, "No that only his kind knew about each other because they keep their kind a secret". Once the other vampires found out he turned me they wanted to challenge me because I was one of the new ones in the family. They came around Marcus house to look for me and fight with me, but Marcus told them if you have a problem with her, you must fight us too. My new family named me Crystal, and they were by my side to fight these other vampires who did not leave me alone. I could not even go out for a rum because they would be watching me. Marcus had to go to work and the family, so they left me home with one of the male family members named Ythies.Ythies was always by my side and no matter where I went, he was there, and Marcus was in constant contact with him. Until one day they came into the house, and they slammed me outside the house and Ythies alerted Marcus and the team ran to the house, but it was far. It was me and Ythies for four other vampires; one woman and three men but we were fighting, and the fight went on for about five minutes until Marcus got there with the family and they fought, and we won. Marcus killed one of the males, so I knew right there and then that this war was not over it was just the beginning. The other vampires left running when Marcus killed one of their teammates and we went back to the house. We know we needed a plan to confront them of they came back which we knew they were coming back because they lost one of their loved ones. We had to come up with a plan and move out of this house for a while until things were calm again. We decided to move to another house in NYC but away from the old neighborhood where the incident happened. Marcus burned the body of the vampire who attacked me and died, and the family helped him burn the body. We kept on living a normal life with precautions because Marcus knew they were coming back with more reinforcement. Other vampires did not like that Marcus turned me and I was strong in the family. I spoke to Marcus and told him I needed to go visit my family and children and he did not want me to go because of the danger I was confronted with in his house. He sent Ythies with me after making up his mind because he feared the thought of loosing me of someone harming me. So, Ythies and I went to Manhattan to see my family and they were so happy to see me. My daughter Christy was surprised to see me, and my oldest son Damien was amazed to see me as well. Jeremia my youngest screamed from joy when he saw me, and my grandson Mykai jumped on top of me when the saw me. Frankie my brother was worried and concerned about me and my where abouts. He asked me why I was so paled and cold, and I told hi it was menopause which he did not believe me. He was worried because I had lost a lot of weight and I was so cold. I told him again that I was fine and he kind of changed the subject. I was there for a few hours, and they asked me about Ythies, and I told them he was a friend of Marcus my boyfriend and they laughed. We played and they offered me food, but I could not eat because I'm in a special diet, but they could not know that because it was a secret. They ordered Dominoes pizza and they were eating with such joy, and I was just looking and remembering when I used to eat food too. The sun was going down and it was getting dark outside you know what people say when the sun goes down danger arises. So Ythies and I decided to leave the apartment to go back to Staten Island in one of the family cars. We drove and noticed we were being followed and we took a different route to lose the car that was following us and then finally we got home. We lost the car that was following us, but we must be careful because we do not want them to know where we are currently residing. Marcus was home and Ythies told him what happened, and he became concerned and told me to stay away from my family for a while just for their safety and I decided he was right, and I called my brother and told him I was going on vacation with Marcus for a few months and he was worried but then he agreed. It was beautiful that life because even though there was always danger to the family because Marcus turned me into a vampire we would go out at night and run together, and we would drink blood together. However, since there was danger in the streets with the other vampires Marcus had to bring extra blood from the blood bank to make sure we did not starve ourselves. Marcus decided to take a few months of vacation from his job just to spend time with me and to make sure that these vampires did not hunt me down again like the last time. We decided to take a vacation to Europe where other vampires lived and the wanted to see if Marcus really tuned me into a vampire so to avoid conflicts Marcus took me to the with the family.

They checked me and smiled because they saw how strong I was, they were impressed. They asked Marcus if I could be of use to them, they are in Europe and Marcus stated, "No". The leaders from Europe became upset and tried to challenge the family so a fight broke loose. Marcus fought with the leader form Europe, and I wanted to help him, but the family stopped me because I was a newborn withing the family and even though I was strong they did not want me to get hurt so I screamed and stated Marcus please do not get hurt and he was just fighting. The other brothers from the Europe family were going to get in but my family was ready for them and Ythies was there too, and he is strong with muscles. It was six of us in the family and about twelve of them so we knew we could not win that fight. So, we decided to leave it one on one with Marcus and Robert which was the name of the one in charge in Europe. They fought for about ten minutes, and we were worried but Marcus new how to fight because he had training from the academy since he was a cop Sargent in the precinct. Roberts brothers stopped the fight and they expressed that we would meet again because they were thrilled by my strength, and they wanted me in their team. But what they did not know and understand was that I was Marcus love, and we were truly hypnotized with each other's love. We could not live without each other and we was going to live together for the rest of our lives. They finally let us go but they said, "We will see you around" and we just walked away and went to our house in Europe. The house was huge, and it had a lot of windows everywhere since we were going to be there for three months, we decided to live comfortably despite of all the drama that have happened in NYC and in Europe. The back yard of the house was just beautiful me and Marcus would go running and bath in the lake right next to our house. We spent those three months so in love it was like a honeymoon to me. Marcus wanted to marry me, but I told him we should wait until things cool off before our wedding. The family was excited that we have decided to get married and they were already making plans especially his parents who were also vampires and part of the family. I loved them because they were sweet to me, and their names were Sasha and Morrow. We were all a team, and they enjoyed my company especially because Marcus loved me. I knew it from the first time I saw Marcus that my life was going to change for ever in a good way. We would play baseball and basketball outside from the house and it was fun especially since we run so fast and jump up high that was the best part of the game. The family protected me because they knew Marcus bit me and that I was liability to the family since they all drink from the blood bank, but Marcus decided to bite me to make me hi woman. We would take turns to go to the blood bank and buy blood for the family since they new my life was in danger all the time. They treated me good and with respect since I was so fragile due to being a new vampire. I was learning different things the family was teaching me for self-defense. We were always practicing how to fight in the back yard to better defend ourselves because Marcus was the one that better knew how to fight since he had experience from the precinct academy and the army. He was my soldier, and I was in love with him. I called my human family from time to time just to check in on them and they were doing well I also sent them money. They missed me and I missed them especially my grandson Mykai who I love very much. I was in my adulthood years, but Marcus looked about 45 years old, but he was about 100's of years including his family. They bite Jeralda many years ago and she is also part of the family. Jeralda was furious and ready to fight always especially for the family. She was planning our wedding with mom, Marcus's mother while we ran errands for the wedding. Since all our friends and family were in NYC, we decided to leave the wedding for when we went back to NYC. Two months has passed, and we are desperate to go back to the city because my human family misses me, and they are worried that something has happed to me. We have not forgotten the problems we left in the city with the other vampires and their crew. We were afraid that they might hurt my human family in the city. I have a big family and they were all calling my brother asking for me I guess they will all be coming to our wedding. The last month we spend it planning for the wedding and sending invitations from Europe to the family. When my brother Frankie saw the invitation, he called me immediately and we spoke for a while and then he congratulated me. He said the family was desperate to see me and to attend to the wedding.

Chapter-4

THE WEDDING

After three long months went by, we decided to go back to the house in NYC and spend some time with my human family. I never stayed to sleep; I just went to visit them because I needed to feed daily from the blood Marcus bought for us. We decided to do our wedding in the cathedral in 114 street and Amsterdam and we paid the priest ahead of time for our wedding. It was amazing my beautiful white dress and my shoes were lovely. I am so excited and the thought of having my human family together with my vampire family was even exciting. We sent out invitations to the Lora family and hidalgo family. We also sent out invitations to the vampire family, the family of Marcus. We were all extremely excited and Jeralda was planning more then everyone for the wedding. The day finally came, and I could not sleep because I was nervous that the human family were going to be together with the vampire family. It was scary just thinking about it because I knew how dangerous and strong vampires can be. My aunts and cousins helped me get dressed and Jeralda and Marcus's mom was also in my dressing room. The room was huge, and my family was so excited. I think they were more excited than I was. I was scared and nervous just thinking that I had to walk the long walk to get to Marcus. Marcus's dad was going to walk with me since my human parents are deceased. We had a photographer that threw beautiful pictures, and he was throwing pictures to the family and the vampire family as well. It was amazing. Everything was beautiful. The cathedral was decorated, and my family was dressed so beautiful it was amazing. The time came and I could not breath. I was so nervous, and I could just see my families smile. The music started and I walked towards Marcus with his dad. We were walking slow, and I was grabbing hi tight because I just wanted to reach to where Marcus was. We walked and the music kept playing and people started clapping I became more nervous. I finally reached towards where Marcus was, and he grabbed my hand. I then had a smile on my face, and we turned around toward the priest. While the pries were reading our vowels me, and Marcus was looking at each other smiling. Everyone in the church was quiet listening and looking at us. It was finally time to kiss after we exchanged rings and we kissed with so much love that everyone started clapping and some were crying. I was amazed by the fact that I'm Marcus wife now. We walked away together, and we hopped in the limousine. People were throwing flowers and rice at us. We were then meeting at this beautiful restaurant where they served us food for all the family and wine and liquor. There was desserts and cake except for blood, but the vampires had their own little celebration after the human party. We planned everything incredibly good, good thing vampires drink alcohol. The celebration ended like at 12pm and then we went to Marcus house to celebrate with blood. We were so joyful and amazed by the fact that everything went well, and the human family were so excited, and they had so much fun to the point of getting drunk. We drank so much blood in Marcus home that I could not drink anymore and then we just stood up talking all night because the next day was our honeymoon. We left to Cancun Mexico for our honeymoon and it was beautiful the house where we were staying and a bed to have the best night ever with Marcus. We rapidly went into the room and kissed with joy, and he touched me softly around my body to the point where I saw stars. He threw me on the bed, and he came on top of me rubbing his body toward mine and making sure I was being pleased. He kissed my entire body and put his tongue everywhere around my body. He then turned me around and continues to kiss my body and all I saw was shining stars everywhere in every kiss that he gave me. It was incredibly wonderful the experience and the moment with Marcus. He skinny body laying toward my body and rubbing on to me. He then turned me around again and finally came on to me and he screamed and so did I from pleasure and joy. We kept making love for hours it was amazing. We finished and went to the lake to go swimming and play for a while. The seven days we lasted in Cancun Mexico was nice and there are no words to describe the beautiful moment me and Marcus spent together. After seven days we decided to go back home to NYC and the first thing I did was to visit my human family to make sure they are well which they were. My grandson is growing and my youngest son jeremia is taller than my oldest son Damien. Frankie is always loved because he is taking care the human family since I cannot live with them anymore because of my special condition. That is why I send Frankie money all the time for the family. Me and Ythies are coming out from my family's home, and we notice a car watching us. We knew that we had unfished business with the vampire that Marcus had killed. So, we knew a big battle was coming. But what they did not know was that we had already planned this battle.

24

Chapter-5

THE BATTLE

Ythies and I immediately got inside the car and drove off, but the problem was they already knew where my human family lived; therefore, they were in danger. Ythies contacted Marcus and Marcus sent vampires to watch my human family outside of the building and cop cars was constantly driving through since Marcus was a cop sergeant. I didn't tell my brother anything except that I was fine and not to come out often which I knew he wasn't going to do. My kids also came out often. Ythies and I drove away to the house but again we had to take another route to avoid the vampires that was following us. Marcus called a few vampires friends that he had and a few vampire cops that were part of his team to be in front of our house just incase they're appeared like they did in the last house. Marcus was worried because we didn't know how many vampires they were, and we didn't know their names just that they were after me (Crystal) because I was a newborn bitten by Marcus. Marcus was the quite a character and he worried so much about me I'm glad I met him. So, we were up all night just waiting and planning the was and outside the house was prepared with traps just incase they came to attack us. Three days passed and nothing happened but after the third day we heard a noise in the background of the house and Marcus receive a phone call from one of our crew members outside. We decided to go outside the entire family and there they were, there were like 20 vampires outside from our house and they told Marcus to give me to them and Marcus told them, you would have to come through us first". Then the fight started it was Marcus, his father, his mother, Ythies, Jeralda, the cops, and Marcus's friends. It was a good 15 of us and we fought with all our strengths and power. We were very powerful especially Marcus who was the fastest. The fight went on for about 30 minutes and many people died including some of our people. After the fight we cleaned up the place by burning all of the bodies including our people because we didn't want the humans to notice our existence. It would be frightening to them to know that vampire do exist. We went home after cleaning up the mess and we spoke about what happened and thanked the vampires that helped us and was in our side. We sent them home and we stood in our house in Staten Island even though we had another house in the lower Manhattan. Ythies and Jeralda mom and dad were fine and so were Marcus. I don't know what I would do if I had lost Marcus of even one of his family members. We knew others like them would come to go after me because the world was getting around that Marcus Bite me, and it was forbitten to bite anyone in the 21 centuries. That why they had the blood banks to avoid any newborn from becoming a vampire. We still have the vampires from Europe who wanted me, and they are twelve, but we are more here in the city. When ever they decide to come for us, we are ready for them because like Marcus said, "they cannot have me". My body doesn't feel the same and I'm a vampire, but something keeps moving inside my stomach. Marcus and I were intimate before he bites me and I'm not sure why my stomach is moving. I must tell Marcus of this because he will get worried if I don't tell him.

THE PREGNANCY

I wait for Marcus to come home from work, and I tell him that something is moving in my stomach. He feels my stomach and is growing very quickly so he gets a doctor to check me. I was scared because I'm a vampire and I didn't want to get noticed but this is family doctor. When the doctor checks my stomach with an ultrasound, he verbalizes to me that I'm pregnant and that the baby is growing fast. He expressed that the baby could be born by next week. I was worried because I was fighting with the stomach not knowing that I was pregnant. Marcus was worried because they never seeing anything like it in centuries and they were scared the baby was going to harm me or that the baby was going to be born a monster. We waited one week before the baby is born and we didn't tell my human family nothing just in case the baby had to be terminated. One week past and I had a C section done by the nice doctor and he took the baby out which was crying so loud, and he had blood all over him and he was a boy. We named him Michael and mom took the baby because I had to heal which I did in second. I had the power of healing which I didn't know until I healed myself. Baby Michael had everything, and he had his own room. He looked human meaning I must have became pregnant when I was still human. We kept the baby a secret because we knew that would bring us problems with the other vampires. Especially, with the vampires from Europe. We didn't know if the baby was going to be good or bad because he was too young, but he was growing fast and he was beautiful just like his mother and dad. Marcus was so happy that he would spend most of his days with the baby. A year passed and Michael looked like he was 5 years old. I had to finally go visit my human family, but we didn't tell them about the baby yet because it was too risky and dangerous. I was in the park with the boys jeremia and Mykai and they had so much fun the I took them back home and went on my way to the house with Ythies. When I got home, we notice an envelop outside of our doors and its an invitation to Europe. They found out about the baby, and they would like to meet him. Marcus became furious and slammed something in the house. Michael was in his room when that happened. Marcus spoke with the family and told them that we cannot go to Europe because they will kill us all over there. Marcus stated they will have to come to NYC if they want to meet Michael. I just thought to myself that this battle never ends because there is always someone that will want to challenge us. The baby is now a threat to the vampires, and I'm scares because I will kill for my son's since Michael is my fourth child that I have now.

Chapter – 6

THE FINAL WAR

We kept living our life as if nothing happened even thought the vampires from Europe wanted to meet Michael. We didn't know how they were going to react when they saw Michael, so we were frightened. The entire family was scared, and we were ready for this war. We are always ready for any war that comes our way. This time Marcus had guns and bombs ready for their arrival because he was scared, they were going to do something to Michael. The war was going to be on the mountains to prevent any humans from getting scared. One more year passed, and we didn't hear anything from the vampires from Europe, but we didn't know what was in Roberts mind. Robert was sneaky and wanted things his way. Marcus had already fought with him once and didn't mind fighting him again. Marcus spoke to all of his friend vampires and cop vampires, and everyone was watching for their arrival even at the airport.

We kept watching and observing until one day Robert appears at the airport and word goes to Marcus. We went deep to the woods and sent word to Robert saying that we were going to be their waiting for them. We waited and we were all present, "The family", Marcus's friends, and cop vampires. Robert approached us so Marcus approached him, and they spoke. Michael was with us just for a while and then one of the vampires was going to take him away for the final war. Roberts asks for Michael and Marcus takes him on his arm to take the baby to Robert just to show him that Michael was not a danger to any of us or the humans. Robert tries to carry him, and Crystal gets out of control and screams, and Marcus is calm, and Michael reaches Robert and Robert carries him. Robert starts playing with the baby and Michael is so innocent that he tries to pull his hair. Robert then tells Messiah one of his crew members to carry Michael so crystal starts running towards Marcus and Robert. Marcus grabs Robert threw his neck and told him, "Give me my son back". Robert replies, "No" so the war starts. Everyone is running toward each other and fighting. All Roberts people was dying and some of our people was dying too. I'm scared because I don't want our family to get hurt. I was fighting like never in my life and I was winning because they had Michael my son and a mother those anything for her son. Marcus was fighting Robert still and they were going at it. I was fighting different vampires and Marcus wasn't using his gun because we had it under control. If more vampires came then we would have to use the guns and bombs. Michael was screaming mom and dad and we were desperate because they had him. They were holding my boy until the fight was over and I was scared. The fight went on until a good 20 minutes and finally Robert didn't want to die because all his vampires were dying so he screamed, "Stop" give them back the baby. Michael came running to us because he was one year old, but he aged like a five-year-old. Michael ran so fast like us, and we were amazed how fast he ran. Even Robert looked at him, but he left and told Marcus, "I will see you again". Marcus told Robert, "You can count on it". They left and we went home but we knew this war wasn't over especially after they saw Michael running like us meaning that Michael was born one of us a vampire, but he was also human. We went home and spoke about this war for days. Marcus decided to go back to work, and I was with the family home taking care of Michael. Michael was growing so fast so we could not put him in a school because it was dangerous, so we decided to hire a home-schooling teacher. Michael was learning a lot, but he was also growing fast so we had to lie to the teacher about his age because she would not believe us if we told her his real age. A few years passed and Michael turned 18 years old but luckily my human family never met him because they would also ask questions about why the baby was growing so fast. We had to finally put him in high school since he stopped growing at the age of 18 years old. Michael was happy to be in high school and he meets a lot of new friends. He also meets a girl in school, and they fall in love. Me and Marcus was afraid this was going to happen, but it happened. They dated and she came to the house to visit, nice young human lady. Me and Marcus was scared that our story was going to repeat. They kept dating and going to school until one day we see Robert again and this time Marcus said he was going to kill him if he touched his son. Robert kept coming back for more from us. Marcus was going to let him have it. Robert then disappeared and never showed his face again

I guess he felt Marcus was going to end his life if he kept messing with his son Michael. We would do a lot of get togethers and we would invite Michael new girl friend to attend, and we would protect her, but our fear was that Michael was going to bite her one day and make her a vampire. Michael graduated from high school and went to college with his girlfriend right beside him. Me and Marcus would never get old, so we were living the life with our friends and family.

THE END

Thank You Note

I want to give a special thanks to my family for being part of my book and life. I want to say thank you to Sean for giving me ideas for my book and to my daughter Christy for listening to my stories and laughing when I was writing my book. A special thanks to all my supporters and friends for reading my books and always saying I'm here for you. I want to thank Frankie, Jeremia, Damien, and Christy for being part of my family and Mykai my grandson you're my heart and love.

Portraits

*I want to thank God for blessing me with my fourth book
and for his wisdom in me!!!*

The Hand

The Family

The Family